How I Learned The Truth About Krampus

Tom Johnstone

How I Learned The Truth About Krampus
by Tom Johnstone

ISBN: 978-1-908125-58-3

Cover Art by David Rix

Publication Date: December 2017

For Mum and Dad. Thanks for everything.

Also for Anna, Katya and Emma. Thanks for everything else. You've made my life more wonderful than it has any right to be.

Thanks to Anna T and Priya for all the help, advice, friendship and encouragement (and books!) you've given me.

Thanks to Tony for making this possible when you told me about this legend, and bacchanalian Krampus Night greetings to the Saint Monday congregation!'

Dear Bella,

I'm writing to try and explain. I know you think I don't care, that I am detached from our terrible loss.

I say 'our' terrible loss. But deep down I suspected that he wasn't mine, so could never quite bond with the child.

I don't mean to be cruel. If I thought I could set things right, I would. There was one thing I might have done to try to remedy the situation, but I think it's futile. As I sit here listening to your anguished sobs filtering down the stairs, I wish I could try anyway, if only to give you some hope of seeing Zac again.

You remember that thing I brought back with me from that trip to Austria? How besotted you were with that carving! I was only half-joking when I gave it to you as a Christmas present. It's certainly the gift that keeps on giving.

One that I'd gladly give back, but I don't think the one I took it from accepts returns.

We scoured the house for the child, then the snow-blanched fields outside, as the bone-bare trees watched. I wondered if Zac's disappearance was a punishment for my theft of the effigy. Might its return act as some kind of ransom?

No. The one who took him got what he came for.

The police have asked me to remain where I am. Not much else I can do really, except write this as I gaze at the wood-burning stove, its black iron frame crouching on four squat legs. The soot-stained glass on its brass-handled door resembles a gaping mouth that opens sideways, making those two art deco crests above the door into eyes and the small central dial the nose.

I'm thinking back to 1991, the second year of my degree, when I first plucked up the courage to get close to you. I wrote you a long letter then too.

Despite initial awkwardness, once we'd broken the ice, we soon found we had a great deal in common.

We'd both lost patience with some of the more mystical ideas espoused by our Head of Department, such as his championing of the quasi-spiritual ideas of Grotowski, of theatre as a kind of masochistic apotheosis of the performer. Artaud's ritualistic 'Theatre of Cruelty' made no sense to either of us, unless grounded in a healthy leavening of Brechtian cynicism, as in Peter Weiss's notorious play *Die Verfolgung und Ermordung Jean Paul Marats, dargestellt durch die Schauspielgruppe des Hospizes zu Charenton unter*

Anleitung des Herrn de Sade. My German studies gave me the opportunity to study this text, more widely known by its contracted title *The Marat / Sade*, in its original form. I also learned that the playwright was a Jew whose family fled the Nazis in the nineteen thirties, much as my grandparents had sought refuge in England after Austria's *Anchluss* with Germany.

It was during this time that I became aware of the role of ritual and folklore in the development of popular street theatre forms such as mummers' plays and *Commedia Dell'Arte*. There is something of this in the mock-solemn execution of the vegetable king in *The Marat / Sade*, as we both agreed during one of our long talks into the small hours. I'm sure you remember those field trips that Des and his colleague Jim Sullivan conducted to places in the West Country where authentic folk rituals still held sway at certain times of the year, partly as a spectacle for the tourists: the burning tar barrels of Ottery St. Mary; The Padstow ''obby 'oss'.

To the boom of drums and the hauntingly repetitive strains of Padstow's traditional May Day song, the ''obby 'oss' lunges to and fro. Those it favours with its dark embrace, who are said to be blessed with pregnancy within a year of being covered: the wide, black disc fringed on all sides by a drape of the same colour; the weird, conical mask jutting from the centre of the disc, representing the rider; the tiny horse's head jutting out of the edge of the disc to the front of the face, a wisp of a tail to his rear. These details combined indicate the grotesque effigy's flimsy resemblance to a horse and rider.

The floor-length drape concealing its wearer, allowing onlookers to forget that there is a man underneath, unless you're a female swallowed up under the black drape and at the tender mercy of the burly fisherman hidden there. I didn't know you very well yet, but when I saw its black skirt pass near you, I shuddered to think of you engulfed in this way. With its red and white stripes and oddly pointed ears, the leering 'head' of the horse's rider reminded me of an African tribal demon mask. Only the eyes peering through the holes were remotely human.

When you emerged from this confined space, this enforced intimacy, you seemed flustered but unharmed. I wanted to go to you, put my arms around you, comfort you, but I didn't know you then. For a moment, you seemed shaken, looked as if you might burst into tears after this ordeal, but instead you broke into a brave grin, to a chorus of lewd cheers from the 'lads' around Mike.

"All very *Wicker Man*", I heard Mike say of the spectacle: *How crass,* I thought, noting he didn't seem the least bit concerned for your well-being. After a while, you grew irritated with me for constantly reminding you of this, protesting that he took you aside later in a quiet moment to ask if you were all right. (*I bet he did,* I've always been tempted to say.) Then you'd add something about how he's the kind of man who conceals his finer feelings and insecurities behind a show of brashness, something he'd never do in front of his private army of mates. More recently you've abandoned this refrain, in favour of the rejoinder that at least he's honest and harmless in his carefree masculinity. One thing I'll never forget is the unmistakeable sound of your throaty laughter as he made the remark. It haunts me still, remembering the hard knot in my gut.

The detective asked me how a child, however small, could vanish from a house where all the doors and windows were locked and bolted? My initial reply was simply to stare at the face of the wood-burning stove. Not the black metal face I mentioned earlier. The one in the glass itself, composed of soot smudges, Turin shroud-faint, but definitely there, as if the metallic face had swallowed another indistinct one in its iron maw.

She glanced helplessly at the poker-faced male officer standing guard by the door.

I kept looking at that stove door. Slightly ajar. Surely a door is either open or shut. But this is not an open-and-shut case. How long had this door been open?

"Not everything was locked and bolted," I said.

She turned to me abruptly, her face eager in the cold winter light from the cottage's small front window.

I nodded towards the stove door.

"What exactly do you mean, Mr Fletcher?" she asked. "Nobody could have –"

"Look inside," I said.

The two officers exchanged glances again. She approached the stove. The hinges creaked as she opened it, poking around inside, releasing a sepulchral cloud of ash, her sooty hand coming out with Zak's dummy.

I knew then she wouldn't give me the benefit of the doubt for much longer. My detachment must seem that of a cold-blooded killer, not a bereaved father's numbness.

I must remain calm. No one had accused me of anything yet.

Nevertheless, how would I tell them what really happened to the child?

Perhaps I should start at the beginning.

Or maybe it would be better to start in the middle: me driving you to the hospital; my grip tightening on your hand as I helped you out of the car when I saw the discarded, broken black umbrella flapping like a smashed-winged crow in the wind; you laughing your throaty laugh through the agonies of the intensifying contractions, pointing out that *you* were the one who was supposed to be nervous! I didn't mention then why I had recently developed such an unreasoning dread of sodden, black umbrellas, the way they flap in the breeze like rotting, wet leaves.

Or shining, leathery wings.

Perhaps if I had warned you of the reasons nine months previously, you wouldn't have been quite so infatuated with the creature that inspired that carving. I might have explained that the effigy was a stylised *representation* of its subject, designed to make the reality it embodied palatable to human eyes.

An image has haunted me since your pregnancy not long after my return from Austria: your face transported by delight, your body transfixed by a corkscrew . . .

Like a butterfly in a Victorian naturalist's nailed-down collection, yet living and screaming in ecstasy.

I thought it must have been a dream, one that repeated itself constantly after I gave you the carving, though never as vividly as that first time, the night after you examined the effigy with such close, rapt attention.

I should show them the carving. But I can't, for the same reason that I can't take it back where it came from.

I destroyed the evidence.

I remember the foul acrid stench – as if I was burning flesh rather than wood. That was nothing to the smell left in the bedroom after that first dream: as if a feral tom cat had marked its territory on our bedspread in the night, then imbued it with the entrails of decomposed birds and small mammals it had mauled, together with the reek of dead leaves long-immersed in putrid, stagnant water. You didn't seem to notice, as you reclined in the afterglow of the kind of languorous, satiated bliss that I could never give you.

Outside the cottage, the snow is deep. The police officers had to trudge over several fields in Wellingtons from their cars in order to get here. So the detective told me. I haven't noticed the weather myself. I've barely looked outside. She glanced pointedly at her boots, drying by the radiator, the flecks of snow slowly turning transparent and trickling onto the flagstone floor. Zac's theoretical kidnapper would have had to do the same, she must have been hinting.

"The one who took him didn't use a car."

"Excuse me?" she said, startled at my sudden breaking of the silence.

"I said, the one who took him didn't use a car."

"You know who took him?"

The smeared grin on the stove door mocked me. The male officer was frowning quizzically at the ash-flecked rubber teat, which he was idly squeezing in his large hand as if it were some macabre executive stress toy.

"What did he use then?" said the male officer, slyly flicking his eyes towards the open stove and the chimney above, "a sledge?"

Ignoring him, she continued: "Mr Fletcher, let's assume that someone, person or persons unknown, came in here last night, despite the doors and windows all being securely locked and bolted, and abducted your son: They would need a car to make their escape surely."

She referred to the child as my son, but I let that pass. I nodded.

"What was that?" she asked.

I must have muttered my reservations aloud. Careless. These days, I'm never quite sure when I'm thinking aloud.

"And you're absolutely sure the doors were all locked and bolted?"

"Apart from the stove door."

You can see it in the male officer's face – he's not bothering to hide it like she is: *Damn nutter, fruitcake, fruit-and-nut-case, did away with his baby son and burnt the body in the oven, then tried to blame it on Santa Claus.*

It wasn't Santa Claus that took him.

Quite the reverse, for jovial old Saint Nicholas is said to leave gifts behind when he comes down the chimney, whereas the intruder I'm talking about stretched itself down the flu-pipe and *took* something, or rather someone, away with him.

I think the police don't believe me. I know you don't, because of the way you ran downstairs and a W.P.C. held you back from attacking me. Such recriminations are understandable. He was your son, not mine. His real father took him back, though I'm still not quite sure how. The flu-pipe on a wood-burning stove is too narrow for an infant.

A fully human infant that is.

"Is this *Krampusnacht* or *Kristallnacht?*" Jim Sullivan wondered aloud.

The rhetorical question was a dig at Des Major. Jim did not share his enthusiasm for folk culture and enjoyed goading Des (whose surname I suspect may have been derived from Meyer, much as mine comes from Fleischer) with its reactionary aspects.

The two lecturers were discussing the grainy film in the Students' Union bar: footage of children in a small Tyrolian market town running from blurry, stick-wielding figures in the horned masks and black capes of Krampus.

I can remember Des's rejoinder, and much of the discussion that followed, pretty much word for word.

"Why? Because it's taking place in a German-speaking country that formed an *Anchluss* with Hitler's Germany? But the Nazis banned *Krampusnacht* celebrations, seeing in them the 'decadence' they despised . . . And what about some of the folk events in this country? Some Catholics might feel pretty uncomfortable in Lewes on November 5th. On the other hand, it's clearly not quite on the same level as an Orange March in Portadown."

"I'm glad you mentioned that," Sullivan replied, "a clear example of how easy it is for unsavoury elements to hide behind so-called folk culture."

"But there is a genuine tradition of ritualised mimesis and collective celebration going back to ancient times," Des argued. "The ''obby 'oss' we saw in Padstow is a primal fertility symbol . . .'"

Suppressed ribald mirth from Mike and his cohorts signalled their growing boredom with the discussion. It reminded me of the time they started yawning and giggling and nudging each other in the middle of a screening of the Peter Brook film of the *Marat / Sade*, as if they were willfully ignorant schoolboys, not undergraduates who had attained the hallowed portals of higher education. I remembered how you'd sympathized with my irritation at this, or seemed to, on that occasion. But this time, as they trooped off to the bar, you left too. I thought you'd just gone to the toilet and would be coming back to join us, but it soon became clear that I was the only one now listening to Major's further thoughts on May Day's origins in the pagan festival of Beltane, Hallowe'en's derivation from *Samhain*, Christmas from Yuletide, and so on.

"You can't get much more primal than Krampus," he went on, lowering his voice conspiratorially, "with his Devil's horns and tail and cloven hooves, with his bundle of sticks for whipping children, his corkscrew phallus and grotesquely extended tongue . . ."

In his lecture, he had already introduced us to Krampus, the dark, folk-devil mirror image of Santa Claus, stick-wielding Old Nick to Saint Nick's carrot, rampaging through European villages every December 5th, dispensing welts and bruises instead of gifts and treats. What seems significant to me now were Major's hints that the figure of Krampus seemed to predate that of Santa Claus. The name derived from the German for 'claws'. One feature of the *Krampusnacht* festivities was that the people of one village would invite a man from a neighbouring village to come into their own in the guise of Krampus, where he was licensed to dispense corporal punishment to the home villagers' children, one of whose fathers would no doubt return the favour. An odd way of encouraging social intercourse between close-knit rural communities, I thought.

"Of course, Krampus is also related to the carnivalesque figure of the Lord of Misrule," Major continued as Sullivan returned from the bar with two pints of ale, "the licenced safety valve for repressed social impulses, in this case during the mid-Winter festivities that correspond to Roman feast of Saturnalia."

"Ah," objected Sullivan, plonking the beers and himself down, "but surely beating your children used to be encouraged not repressed during the heyday of Krampus."

"Yes, there are certain problems in casting the Devil as the enforcer of discipline," Major conceded, "but then that's always been one of the problems with the idea: The Being responsible for tempting humankind into Sin is also in charge of punishing us. Poacher turned game-keeper, if you will . . . And Krampus *only* performs the function of punishment . . ."

He continued in this vein, but the sound of your throaty laughter from the bar broke my concentration. There you were in smiling and animated conversation with Mike. He'd steered you a little distance away from his entourage, creating a little bubble of intimacy. They seemed to be complicit in this, as if he'd instructed them to ease his conquest. That's how it seemed to me. Or perhaps my memory has exaggerated it retrospectively. I wonder if this is when the two of you became close.

I fixed my gaze on the posters, one of which was for one of the *Nightmare on Elm Street* movies, the other showing a young woman using a scaffolding pole to fend off a baton-wielding riot policeman.

Perhaps Jim Sullivan saw the direction of my gaze. I could smell his yeasty breath, see the froth clinging to his straw-coloured beard as he nudged me:

"I think Krampus could make a come-back in this Age of Austerity, eh, Dan? After all," he added pointedly, "Mussolini named his movement after the Latin word *Fasces*, the bundle of sticks used by the Romans to quell riots. *Bundle of sticks . . .*"

Later, I could see what he meant: he was alluding to Krampus's traditional weapons of chastisement. At the time I just nodded blankly. Out of the corner of my eye, I thought I could see Mike reaching out to caress your shining red hair. I thought of a looter sizing up copper piping for its scrap metal value.

That night, as I lay awake and tried to banish this image from my mind, it all seemed to come together. Two icons of the age: a child-murdering demon with razor-sharp claws for fingers and an oddly Germanic name (beginning with a 'K'!); a system that destroyed children's future and responded to the demands of the young for a better life with the riot cop's baton.

Thus the beginnings of my uncompleted MA thesis began to take shape.

I have spent long enough on these events preceding my trip to Austria. During many of them, you were there! I don't need to remind either of us how your fling with Mike played out, though when his dalliance with your best friend came to light I tried to comfort you without displaying any *schadenfreude*.

I think the police are going to arrest me for killing the boy when they've finished their search of the surrounding countryside. So I can spend no more time on how, little by little, we grew closer; how I gently prised you away from his influence, won you over from the Dark Side, I like to think. We became engaged following our graduation, with the marriage set for the following June. In the intervening winter, I arranged a visit to the University of Graz to research my paper on the cultural history of *Krampusnacht*.

In hindsight, our engagement may have been over-hasty, me too eager, you still licking your wounds. When I prepared to leave at the end of November, I was not unduly concerned at your remaining behind in Exeter, where Mike also hung around. As you yourself insisted, you were 'over him' by then. With the blessing of Des Major and the help of my connections in the German language department at Exeter, I arrived at the Karl-Franzens-Universitat Graz, where a young woman who introduced herself as Claudia ushered me into office of Dr Klaus Baumgarter, lecturer in Social and Cultural Anthology.

Let me just add that nothing of any significance happened between Claudia and me, though you and I agreed to keep our relationship open during our brief separation. However, there were moments during my stay when whispers of intimacy did hang breathless between myself and the assistant to Dr Baumgarter.

I'll try to recount my visit to Austria in as much detail as I can, as you weren't with me during this time.

"Welcome to Graz, Herr Fletcher," began Baumgarter in English. "Is this your first visit to Austria? I understand that you have some family connections with our country . . ."

I was gratified that he didn't consider the matter too sensitive to bring up.

I nodded slowly, then replied in German.

"My grandparents moved to England . . . before the war. I am the first one in my family to return, out of the ones who left."

I didn't like to mention what happened to the ones who refused or didn't manage to get out.

"Indeed," he said. He sat at his desk, his large, friendly eyes and eager toothy smile waiting for me to break the uncomfortable silence, perhaps with further details about my background. When none were forthcoming, he glanced at Claudia, who asked if I'd like to sit down.

"There has never been a reason to return," I added, taking the offered chair, "until now."

"Not even to help you improve your German?"

"My grandfather gave me some personal tuition," I replied. "And I have also pursued extensive reading of German texts while pursuing my degree, including the book you co-edited on traditional folk performance customs in the Alpine-Adriatic-Danube region."

"You must be the only one!" he said, and he laughed, showing his large teeth. "But your spoken German is excellent. Your grandfather must have taught you well."

I smiled, then went on.

"I was a little disappointed to find none of H. Scherzinger's work on the Krampusnacht festivities in the book though."

Dr Baumgarter scratched his large, fleshy nose. He was finding it harder to sustain his Cheshire Cat's grin.

"Yes, I'm afraid we had to exclude Holger's paper from the book at the last minute," he said.

"Oh really, why was that?" I asked.

Dr Baumgarter shifted uncomfortably in his seat. Claudia approached the desk with a tray of coffee and pastries.

"We, the editorial team, felt that . . . Thank you, Claudia. We felt that his work had strayed into the territory of what one might call cryptozoology. Coffee?"

I thanked him, then went on: "My tutor said that Scherzinger was the only academic who was carrying out a serious study of the Krampus phenomenon. When I couldn't find any of his work in England, I was hoping you might have something I could look at."

"Sugar?" asked Baumgarter, then replied. "No. I'm afraid his papers were shredded. By accident."

"Right," I said. "But what's the link between Krampus and the Abominable Snowman?"

Baumgarter smiled briefly and thinly, this time not showing his teeth.

"He claims to have found one: a missing link." After a snort at his own joke, he sighed before setting out the theory that he found so obviously distasteful. "He believes that Krampus is based on some kind of Alpine hominid survival. He calls it," and here Baumgarter paused for mock-dramatic effect, "*Homo Saturnalius!*"

"I see," I said, finishing my coffee, digesting both Baumgarter's words and the pastries. Claudia began clearing the refreshments away, staring intently at the desk as she did so, colouring slightly. Then I said: "I came here to research the traditions around *Krampusnacht*. If I can't read Scherzinger's paper on the subject, perhaps I could speak to him in person. Do you have his contact details?"

The silence was broken when the loaded tray slipped from Claudia's hands with a crash. I jumped to my feet.

"Let me help," I offered. I began clearing up broken crockery as Baumgarter gently led her to the door.

"Thank you," said Baumgarter. "Claudia and Holger were . . . close. She has taken his disappearance badly."

"Ah," I said. He had answered my enquiry as to the possibility of an interview with Scherzinger.

"When she has recovered her composure, Claudia will escort you to your quarters," he continued. "I am sorry that you couldn't meet him, but shortly you will at least be able to experience the Krampus parade at first hand, here in Graz."

The snow ploughs were already in operation, as the taxi took Claudia and me to the student accommodation just off Bergmanngasse. She showed me into the small, anonymous dormitory-type room. Thinking of you, I suddenly felt horribly alone. She didn't look too happy either. I asked her if she wanted to stay for a moment and have a cup of tea before going back out into the twilit winter afternoon.

She said she ought to be getting back before it got dark, and made to leave.

"I'm sorry if my questions to Dr Baumgarter upset you," I said.

She paused in the doorway, turned her head. Her dark eyes met mine.

"How important is it for you to speak to Holger, Mr Fletcher?" she asked.

I shrugged.

"There's little point in my being here unless I do. He's supposed to be the main authority."

"That's not what Dr Baumgarter thinks." Her eyes flashed; she marched back into the room, and stood gazing out of the window into the darkness only broken by large blobs of snow, pale fingertips that brushed against the glass. "I think I know where to find him, Mr Fletcher, but I need help."

"Where did he go, Claudia?" I asked.

"He went west, to find *Homo Saturnalius*. He said while researching his paper that he'd heard of villages in the Tyrol where the Krampus festival had died out: children admitted to hospital with strange welts and lacerations, others going missing altogether. And all around December 5th."

"*Krampusnacht*," I murmured. I could see her face reflected in the window pane, her eyes deep hollows.

"These, the missing ones, he began calling the 'Children of Krampus'." She turned around with a sad smile. "That's when Dr Baumgarter thinks he began to lose it: 'a promising academic with a bright future, turned sensation-seeking monster hunter'. Those were his words."

Behind her, in the windows, I could see my own face smiling back from the darkness where the snow fingers blindly groped at the panes, leaving melt prints. For a moment I thought I saw two points of light above the face, but they couldn't have been stars on such a night.

"Will you help me, Mr Fletcher?" she asked.

"Daniel," I said. "I'll try."

The next day, on the early morning train to Innsbruck, I stared out of the window at the flint-and-snow lattice of the Alps.

"It is beautiful," I said.

"And your grandfather didn't want to return?" Claudia asked, her hand gently brushing my forearm.

"Perhaps he did," I smiled. "Maybe that's why he kept up his German for all those years."

We hired a car in Innsbruck. Claudia drove. We visited every village, every small provincial market town in Tyrol. In those where there were no signs that the inhabitants were preparing for

Krampusnacht, we stopped and made inquiries, showing any locals we met Claudia's photo of Holger's rugged, fair-haired features. It may seem odd that we selected these places, rather than those where blackened effigies of the horned demon already festooned the shops and *bierkellers*; yet according to Claudia, Holger's theory was that through *Krampusnacht*, people used the image of Krampus to ward off the real thing: repelling Evil with its own image, like the custom of lighting ghostly Jack O' Lanterns at Hallowe'en to keep away evil spirits. It did seem as if those places gearing up for *Krampusnacht* revelry boasted happy, healthy-looking children from some Alpine picture postcard, rosy-cheeked and hurling snowballs; whereas the few youngsters I saw in the places where the custom had atrophied looked wan, pale, listless and frightened of their own shadows.

It was one of these unfortunates that led me to the carving. He didn't say much. He seemed in a dreadful hurry to get home before nightfall. He must have been about thirteen, with that awful cracked voice that comes to boys with puberty. When he told us of the stranger from the city, who asked about a network of caves in the foothills nearby, Claudia and I exchanged glances. I could see welts on his neck. I don't need to describe them to you: you've already seen similar ones on Zac.

"It's getting dark," said Claudia.

I nodded and suggested we find somewhere

to stay for the night. In the end, we were able to hire a hunting lodge. The owner always found it difficult to let this one, right near the foothills of the Alps. When we mentioned our interest in the caves, he told us that there had been a history of accidents and odd sightings there. He mentioned tales of those that walked like men, yet were something else entirely.

"People have seen hairier men than him," he joked, pointing at the photo of Holger that Claudia was holding. At least, I think that's what he said. There was something else he said that I could have misunderstood: something about "men with wings".

"Did he stay in the hunting lodge?" asked Claudia.

"Oh no," said the landlord. "He had a tent with him. It was still quite warm then. I remember seeing him going that way when I was doing some work on the lodge. Didn't see him come back though."

The following day we found Holger's tent.

That wasn't all we found.

We set off at first light, following the directions the landlord had given us, under protest and with many misgivings about our safety. The milky-grey light gave the winding mountain path a forbidding quality, and it was getting darker. Snowstorm clouds were building up, and I was beginning to wonder how Claudia had managed to talk me into this. I had thought of it as research, and I had certainly seen at first-hand how various different Alpine communities prepared to celebrate *Krampusnacht*, though it was still a couple of days until December 5th.

As I heard scree rattling down the slopes near our feet, I thought how far removed this strange adventure was from how I'd imagined I'd be spending this week: sitting in a nice, warm, air-conditioned library, leafing through a few books and pamphlets, maybe watching the gaudy and grisly yet basically unthreatening Krampus parade in Graz.

Claudia was trying to hold her map steady against the strengthening winds, buffeting her with the first snowfall of the day, when I spotted the blue tatters.

"Look!" I said, pointing at the remains of the tent.

Her face fell as she saw it. She folded up the map.

"The wind?" I wondered aloud.

"The wind couldn't do that," she said. "It's been slashed to ribbons."

Inside was a camera, a lighter, a camping stove, a sodden sleeping bag, a notebook also sodden so as to be illegible, and the strangest and most obscenely beautiful wood carving I have ever seen. I don't need to describe it to you: I'm only too aware of the spell it cast on you. I too was bewitched by it. The German language has a word for the feeling it inspired in me: *Ehrfurcht*, a reverence for that which we cannot understand.

Though it shared the horns and hooves and bat-like wings of the images of Krampus decorating many of the Alpine villages we'd passed through, it had none of their ugly grotesquery, its chiselled features almost delicate beneath the over-hanging brow, which made the gleeful malevolence of the expression seem even more chilling. The eyes were almost human. As I knelt in the ruins of Holger Scherzinger's tent, I gazed at the jet-black effigy in wonder and rapture, the heavy, wind-driven snowflakes beating on my back like a warning.

And it spoke to me.

Claudia's cries seemed muffled by the snow, just as her jerking form was distorted by its thick precipitation. Maybe that's why, when her remains tumbled off the edge of the precipice, I thought I saw a figure behind her, dragging her into air: the wings like flapping, leathery umbrellas; all I saw of the face was a glimpse of a long pink tongue dangling from the charcoal features, eyes strangely human, as if peering through the eyeholes of a mask. Then the thing rose high into the mountains, leaving behind a feral tom-cat, charnel house odour.

To my shame, all I could think was: *It didn't see me, I'm spared!*

Grabbing the carving, I headed back to the lodge. Somehow, I'm still not quite sure how, I made it back to Graz.

Now do you see why I dread umbrellas?

I booked myself an earlier flight. It wouldn't have helped Claudia if I'd hung around to answer awkward questions about her last known whereabouts (showing me to my digs), or to try and explain to the *polizei* that I had seen her shredded and casually tossed aside by some primal, winged man-beast. They would simply conclude that I had pushed her over the edge, driven to homicidal rage by guilt at my betrayal of you with her, something I say again never happened. Not really.

However, I am now faced with the prospect of explaining Zac's disappearance to the authorities here in similar terms, further complicated by my suspicions about his paternity. When I hint to the police about what I believe his origins are and where I believe he's gone, I am rewarded with pitying looks from the female officer and less pitying ones from her male subordinate.

I suspect that they are growing impatient with my elliptical responses to their polite questions, and will soon ask me to accompany them to the station in order to put the conversation on a more formal footing. So I need to be brief in concluding this account – well, briefer than I have been so far.

So I won't dwell too long on the details of our wedding the following June: my grandfather beating his stick on the floor from his wheelchair to order my father to attend to his wants; your father's amusing speech: "When my daughter told me her fiancé was Jewish, I said . . . 'Never mind'!" to general hilarity, on his side of the family anyway. My main memory of the day was wondering where you were for most of the reception. Mike was nowhere to be seen either. On your insistence, we had invited him.

I don't mention this in order to cast myself as some sort of saint. When I said nothing happened with Claudia, I was being a little dishonest. That night in the one-room cabin threw us together, and after some food and wine, exhausted we collapsed on the sofa and suddenly found ourselves in an embrace, though guilt meant I was unable to surrender to the moment, and I went to bed alone on the camp bed while Claudia remained on the sofa, asleep, I assumed. I closed my eyes. I heard a rustle, which might have been her removing her clothes, or perhaps settling down to sleep.

"Claudia," I whispered. "Claudia."

There was no reply.

Our ascent of the mountain the following day was marred by mutual awkwardness and unspoken bitterness. Perhaps that was why I was crouching in the ruined tent when the creature attacked Claudia. If it hadn't been for that, perhaps I might have been able to save her.

The carved effigy I discovered in that tent was a source of endless fascination and delight to you when I presented it to you on my return. You chuckled at the bizarre, spiral shape of the long, pointed genitals, and stroked it in mock tenderness. I joined in your laughter, though your behaviour unsettled me.

It was about two months later that the dreams started. At least I think they were dreams, though sometimes I wonder if I was awake. If I still had the carving, I would ask it: it was always too willing to venture opinions on matters of the heart, telling me that you had been chosen to carry his child, until eventually I got sick of its garrulousness and burnt it, burnt it so that the evil fumes stung my nostrils and I thought I'd never be rid of the smell!

I burnt it to stop it talking to me.

But it carried on.

In the dreams (if they were dreams) I saw you happily straddling that fiend, spinning round and round and up and down, riding his corkscrew cock. I wondered how you could do it, whether he'd somehow drugged or hypnotised you so that you couldn't see that dreadful pink-tongued broken umbrella face, those beating wings, ram's horns, fish-hook claws and cloven hooves. But then I saw that he was wearing a mask, different masks. Sometimes he wore Mike's face, that cocksure cock of the walk. Sometimes he wore my face, and was I watching then, or was I actually in his body – if so he was helping me with my erectile dysfunction!

That was before the wedding. During the reception I heard people wondering if you were pregnant, the same insufferable busy-bodies asking each other where you were, where Mike was, and giving me pitying looks to rub my nose in it. That really put the icing on the wedding cake! Or maybe I only imagined I heard them, maybe it was really that damned carving: I told you how chatty that thing was.

It was to me anyway. Did it never talk to *you*, tell you how lucky you were to get the chance to bring forth the spawn of *Homo Saturnalius*?

But you've never accepted that, Bella, always insisted the child was mine. Maybe you really believed it. I know better. That wedding in June, it really put lead in my pencil: for the first time we were able to have full physical relations, for the first time I'd thrown off my cuckold's horns and we'd finally put your dalliance with Mike behind us.

Isaac Mordechai Fletcher was born on December 5ᵗʰ, barely six months after the wedding, but nine months after I last saw you pirouetting on the umbrella man, and within a year of you first setting eyes on that carving. You always said he looked like me, but babies all look the same when they're that age, don't they? And there were other things that made me wonder, such as the strangely shaped welts and lacerations that appeared on him. No doubt you now blame these on me, but when people express disbelief that a father could do such a thing to his son, I say that they should read about Krampus, a loving father that leaves the signs of his affection on his children.

And those that agree with you about the resemblance should look at the boy's feet. At first I thought it was an effect of the nine-month long immersion in amniotic fluid that made them look like that. Just as it made the rest of his skin so purple and wrinkly, like the skin of someone that has spent too long in the bath. Eventually the baby's skin contracted to fit him, but he still looked alien with his deep black eyes and the white plastic clip attached to the withering scrap of umbilical cord.

The police have now told me I don't have to say anything but what I do say may be given in evidence, and have mentioned the possibility of extradition to Austria on an outstanding Interpol warrant, in addition to the charges I face in this country.

They say they have found traces of Zac's DNA inside the wood-burning stove. Do they think I don't know the difference between wood and flesh – even though the wooden carving gave off the stench of burning flesh when I threw it in there? If you think about it, burning the boy's body would have been the last thing I'd have done: the body would have proved the truth of my story, proved that he's no son of mine. I try to explain to them though they won't listen: if I'd done that, the plastic dummy would have melted, which *proves* that it fell out of his gums into the *unlit* burner as something dragged him up the flu-pipe!

I remember reading somewhere that some of our ancestors had a greater proportion of cartilage in their bones than we do: if this trait had survived in '*Homo Saturnalius*', it would have given the species extra elasticity. Just a thought.

I wonder if there's a missing link with leathery wings, perhaps related somehow to the bat. Yes, I know it sounds insane, but is it any crazier than what they're accusing me of? If only I could get hold of Scherzinger's papers! I wonder if there's something about those DNA samples they don't want to tell the world.

That Zac is nowhere to be found is deeply frustrating: if they could only look at the boy's remains, they could look at his feet, and see that the gap between the middle and second toes on each foot is considerably longer than those between the other toes, giving his feet the appearance of cloven hooves, the feet he got from the father that I believe came down the chimney to claim him.

In my mind's eye, I see those human eyes I saw on the thing in Austria, and they look like Zac's.

And that's the story, as I experienced it. I know it's been difficult for you, losing Zac and everything, but you must understand it's been hard for me too. I know I sometimes find it hard to express my emotions in an upfront way. Setting them down on paper is the best way for me to do it. So I hope that you read this letter, and that it makes everything clearer.

That is all; except to say that I still love you, despite everything that's happened, and I think that on some level you still love me too, though perhaps you are finding it hard to admit this to yourself at present.

I trust that reading this will make it easier.
Your loving husband,
Daniel.

www.ingramcontent.com/pod-product-compliance
Lightning Source LLC
Chambersburg PA
CBHW032045180726
48284CB00008B/2766